THE SLEEPOVER

MICHAEL REGINA

RAZORBILL

DEDICATED TO RUBY WARD

RAZORBILL

An imprint of Penguin Random House LLC, New York

First published in the United States of America by Razorbill,
an imprint of Penguin Random House LLC, 2021

Copyright © 2021 by Michael Regina

Visit us online at penguinrandomhouse.com.

Library of Congress Cataloging-in-Publication Data
Names: Regina, Michael, author, illustrator.
Title: The sleepover / Michael Regina.
Description: New York: Razorbill, 2021. | Audience: Ages 8–12. | Summary: Matt's friends plan a fun sleepover to try and cheer him up after he falls into a deep grief over the death of his nanny, but the sleepover quickly takes a turn when they realize the family's new nanny may be an actual monster.
Identifiers: LCCN 2021008380 | ISBN 9780593117347 (hardcover) | ISBN 9780593117361 (trade paperback) | ISBN 9780593117354 (ebook) | ISBN 9780593352908 (ebook) | ISBN 9780593352915 (ebook) Subjects: LCSH: Graphic novels. | CYAC: Graphic novels. Friendship—Fiction. | Monsters—Ficiton. | Grief—FIction. | Sleepovers—Fiction. | Nannies—Fiction. | Horror stories. Classification: LCC PZ7.7.R4456 Sl 2021 | DDC 741.5/973—dc23
LC record available at https://lccn.loc.gov/2021008380

ISBN 9780593117347 (hardcover) | ISBN 9780593117361 (paperback)

Manufactured in China

The artwork for this book was created digitally.

1 3 5 7 9 10 8 6 4 2

TPLF

Design by Michael Regina | Text set in Milk Mustache

MATT, RUBY'S CHOCOLATE-COVERED POPCORN IS AMAZING!

RIGHT?! I DON'T KNOW WHY MY SISTER RUINS HERS BY PUTTING ALL THAT SALT ON IT.

BECAUSE JUDY IS A GROSS SEVEN-YEAR-OLD.

DO WE HAVE TO KEEP WATCHING SCARY STUFF EVERY TIME WE HAVE A SLEEPOVER?

DON'T WORRY. WE CAN WATCH SOMETHING FUNNY AFTER THIS IF YOU WANT . . .

THANKS, MATT.

BUT I BROUGHT A BUNCH OF HORROR MOVIES WE STILL NEED TO WATCH!

BOOM!

WHOA, THAT THUNDER WAS SO CLOSE!

THAT WAS SO SCARY!

HA! CHARLIE JUMPED!

SHUT UP, MARIO!

WHOA! JUDY, IT'S OK! I'VE GOT YOU.

MATTHEW.

YOU CAN'T HAVE THE TV ON DURING THE STORM.

YOU BOYS TURN IT OFF AND COME SIT IN THE LIVING ROOM WITH ME.

YES, RUBY.

COME ON, GUYS. LET'S GO.

WHAT?! BUT WE HAVE TO FINISH THE EPISODE!

YOU KNOW THUNDERSTORMS SCARE RUBY.

TEO, WE'RE INSIDE AND SAFE! THIS MAKES NO SENSE. SHE'S LUCKY I LIKE HER SO MUCH.

BOOM!

THANK YOU, BOYS, FOR SITTING WITH ME.

I'M SORRY TO MESS UP YOUR SLEEPOVER.

IT'S OK, RUBY! WE'RE HAPPY TO STAY WITH YOU.

SAYS YOU! YOU'RE JUST SCARED OF THE SHOW.

SO?! WHAT IF I AM?

DO YOU GUYS THINK THE JERSEY DEVIL IS REAL, LIKE IN *THE X-FILES*?

YEAH, MAYBE! I'M SURE ALL KINDS OF CREATURES ARE OUT THERE. I BET BIGFOOT IS REAL TOO!

PFFT WHO NEEDS EITHER OF THEM WHEN WE HAVE A MONSTER RIGHT HERE IN OUR OWN BACKYARD?

DO YOU THINK IT'S TRUE, RUBY?

I DON'T KNOW ABOUT MONSTERS, BUT THOSE WOODS AREN'T SAFE.

YOU KIDS SHOULD NEVER WANDER INTO THERE.

YOU EVER WONDER WHY THERE'S SO MANY RAVENS BACK THERE, OR WHY IT'S FENCED OFF WITH BARBED WIRE?

UH, BECAUSE IT'S THE WOODS?

NO! IT'S BECAUSE THOSE WOODS ARE HAUNTED! THE BIRDS COMMUNE WITH DARK SPIRITS AND THE WITCH IS THEIR QUEEN!

I DON'T LIKE WITCHES!

OH, IT'S SILLY STORIES. DON'T LISTEN TO HIM.

DUDE, STOP IT! YOU'RE SCARING JUDY!

NO, IT'S NOT! LOTS OF KIDS HAVE GONE MISSING IN THIS NEIGHBORHOOD! SHE LURES THEM INTO THE WOODS, AND IF YOU GO IN THERE, YOU'RE MARKED. THEN SHE HAUNTS YOU!

BESIDES, THAT'S ALL MADE UP ANYWAYS!

W-WHAT DOES SHE LOOK LIKE?

PEOPLE SAY THEY'VE SEEN SOME KIND OF GIANT BIRD CREATURE. LIKE SHE SHAPE-SHIFTS OR SOMETHING.

YES! BUT SHE CAN ONLY TURN INTO A BIRD MONSTER AFTER THE WITCHING HOUR, AT MIDNIGHT . . .

WHEN SHE HUNTS AND EATS YOU!

BWAHAHAHA!

BOOM!

CLICK!

OH NO! THE WITCH IS AT THE DOOR!

HELLO, EVERYONE!

GOODNESS, THE STORM IS CRAZY OUT THERE! I SEE RUBY MADE YOU ALL WAIT IT OUT WITH HER.

IT'S JUST MOM, JUDY! SHE'S HOME FROM WORK EARLY.

YEAH, MS. RUSSO. WE'RE MISSING THE END OF *THE X-FILES* EPISODE!

WELL, SINCE I'M HOME NOW, I THINK YOU'RE OK TO GO BACK TO IT.

REALLY?!

COME ON! LET'S GO!

YOU'RE THE BEST, MS. R!

GET THE POPCORN! MAYBE WE CAN CATCH THE LAST FEW MINUTES!

YOU OK? SORRY MARIO SCARED YOU.

I'M OK. THANKS!

REMEMBER, YOU GUYS CAN'T STAY UP TOO LATE TONIGHT. WE HAVE TO HIT THE ROAD EARLY TOMORROW.

BUT, MOM!

WHAT'S THE POINT OF A SLEEPOVER IF WE CAN'T STAY UP ALL NIGHT?!

YOU ASKED TO SEE YOUR FRIENDS BEFORE WE LEAVE FOR VACATION AND I LET YOU. NOW I NEED YOU TO GO TO BED SOON!

MATTHEW, LISTEN TO YOUR MOMMA.

FINE.

I WISH YOU WERE GOING WITH US, RUBY. YOU ALWAYS COME . . .

I KNOW. ME TOO. JUST CAN'T THIS TIME. I'M SURE MY OWN MOMMA WILL BE GLAD TO HAVE ME AT HOME TO HELP HER FOR A FEW DAYS, THOUGH.

COUGH

COUGH

RUBY?! ARE YOU OK? YOU'VE BEEN COUGHING A LOT LATELY!

RUBY'S GONNA LOVE THIS!

FEAR CRYSTAL

MATTHEW! I SAID COME HELP US!

I'M COMING.

BEEP

HI, SHERYL. THIS IS TRICIA SIMMONS, RUBY'S MOTHER . . .

GRRR! COME ON!

I HATE LEAVING YOU A MESSAGE LIKE THIS, BUT . . .

JUDY, ARE YOU SURE YOU DON'T NEED HELP?

YES, PLEASE HELP!

I DIDN'T KNOW HOW TO REACH YOU AND . . . OH, SHERYL . . .

IT'S RUBY . . .

JOVI

... THE ONES WE LOVE NEVER LEAVE US. THAT THE LIGHT OF THEIR LIVES STAYS IN OUR HEARTS IF WE LET IT ...

I BELIEVE THAT'S TRUE. BUT THAT DOESN'T STOP THE PAIN FROM SWALLOWING YOU ...

WE HAVE TO FIGHT TO NOT RETREAT, ALONE, INTO OUR PAIN ...

AND LOSE EVERYTHING AND EVERYONE ...

. . . GRIEF IS HARD . . .
IT CAN EAT YOU
UP INSIDE . . .

MAKE SURE YOU
CHANGE OUT OF
YOUR NICE
CLOTHES.

TO GET THROUGH
THIS TIME . . .

. . . WE'RE GOING TO
HAVE TO BE THERE
FOR EACH OTHER . . .

NO MATTER
WHAT.

KRAA!

TWO WEEKS LATER

I KNOW AND I'M SORRY.

I'M DOING THE BEST I CAN.

I *AM* LOOKING FOR SOMEONE NEW TO WATCH THE KIDS SO I CAN GET BACK TO WORK, BUT IT HASN'T BEEN EASY . . . OR WHAT I CAN AFFORD.

NO, I'M NOT SAYING YOU DON'T PAY ME ENOUGH.

JUST, PLEASE, GIVE ME A COUPLE MORE DAYS. I CAN'T LOSE THIS JOB.

TODAY?! *SIGH* YOU KNOW THAT'S ALMOST IMPOSSIBLE--

I UNDERSTAND. I'LL FIGURE SOMETHING OUT.

SOB

HELP WANTED

911-555-1970

THEY WON'T. NOT IF SHE WENT INTO THE WOODS. COPS NEVER GO IN THERE . . . THEY KNOW THE WITCH IS REAL.

DUDE, THE WITCH ISN'T REAL!

TELL THAT TO BETHANY.

WITCH!

AHH! IT'S ONE OF HER MINIONS!

GET OUT OF HERE!

UH . . . DID THAT BIRD SPEAK?

YEAH! APPARENTLY RAVENS CAN DO THAT!

THEY'RE REALLY SMART, ACTUALLY. THEY CAN REMEMBER PEOPLE'S FACES AND EVEN HOLD GRUDGES.

THAT'S TERRIFYING.

WHEN DID YOU BECOME A BIRD EXPERT?

I STARTED LOOKING INTO THEM AFTER ALL THAT WITCH TALK.

YOU'RE SUCH A WEIRDO.

COME ON, YOU GUYS.

TEO, WHERE ARE YOU GOING?

WE'RE GOING TO HELP MATT GET OUT OF THIS FUNK.

MATTHEW! STOP RUNNING THROUGH THIS HOUSE!

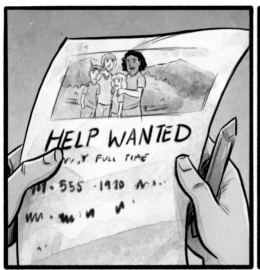

HELP WANTED

M...X FULL TIME

707-555-1920 M...

I'M JUST EXCITED! I NEED TO GET MY BAIT.

DON'T YOU TAKE ALL MY BREAD!

FOUR MONTHS AGO

IT'S THE FIRST FISHING DAY OF SUMMER, RUBY!

WHAT'S THAT GOT TO DO WITH YOU RUNNING THROUGH THE HOUSE?!

BABY, HOLD ON.

WHAT?

29

WELL, WILL YOU PLAY WITH ME INSTEAD?

SIGH

I DON'T FEEL LIKE IT TODAY, OK?

JUST LEAVE ME ALONE--

MATTHEW!

DON'T BE A SCAREDY-CAT. YOU TRUST ME, RIGHT?

YEAH . . .

THEN COME WITH ME.

UM . . .

OK.

WE'LL BE FAST.

DO YOU THINK IT'S RUBY'S GHOST?

NO. GHOSTS AREN'T REAL!

THEN WHAT IS IT?

CRUNCH!

WHOA!

WHAT IS THAT?!

IT'S A SNAKE'S SKELETON. I THINK IT'S THE SAME ONE--

MATTHEW!

THERE IT IS AGAIN!

I WANT TO GO HOME!

DO YOU THINK ALL OF THOSE BIRDS WERE FROM THE WITCH?

NO, STOP TALKING ABOUT HER!

BUT WHAT ABOUT THE VOICES?

WE JUST IMAGINED IT! REMEMBER, DON'T TELL--

MOM?

OH, KIDS! YOU'RE BACK! I HAVE SOMEONE FOR YOU TO MEET.

I KNOW. ME NEITHER.

WHY DID YOU TAKE OUR FAMILY PICTURE FROM THE LIVING ROOM?

IT REMINDS ME OF HER.

I DON'T WANT TO FORGET HER.

MATTHEW . . . YOU KNOW I HAVE TO GO BACK TO WORK. WE NEED SOMEONE TO WATCH YOU AND YOUR SISTER.

BUT WHY HER, MOM?

WHAT'S WRONG WITH HER?

SOMETHING ISN'T RIGHT ABOUT HER.

WHAT IF SHE'S EVIL?

43

THAT'S RIDICULOUS. YOU WATCH TOO MANY SCARY MOVIES.

WHO IS SHE, MOM? SHE JUST SHOWED UP AND YOU TRUST HER WITH US? WHERE DID SHE EVEN COME FROM?

WE DON'T KNOW ANYTHING ABOUT HER AND YOU'RE JUST LEAVING US WITH THIS LADY?

THAT'S NOT FAIR!

WE'VE HAD ADS OUT FOR WEEKS SINCE RUBY DIED. IT'S NOT BEEN EASY TO FIND SOMEONE NEW.

AND NO, WE'LL NEVER BE ABLE TO FIND SOMEONE LIKE RUBY. BUT I NEED YOU TO LISTEN TO ME.

WE HAVE TO GIVE MISS SWAN A CHANCE AND SHE NEEDS TO START TODAY . . . BECAUSE IF I CAN'T GET BACK TO WORK, I'M GOING TO LOSE MY JOB, AND . . .

THEN WE WON'T HAVE A HOUSE TO LIVE IN.

DO YOU UNDERSTAND?

KNOCK! KNOCK!

44

IS EVERYTHING OK?

YES, I'M SORRY.

MATTHEW IS JUST HAVING A HARD TIME ACCEPTING CHANGE . . .

I GET IT . . .

CHILDREN CAN BE AN UNRULY BUNCH. CARRIED BY THEIR EMOTIONS. BUT I'M SURE WITH SOME TIME TOGETHER . . .

WE'LL BE FAST FRIENDS.

SPEAKING OF FRIENDS, CHARLIE JUST CALLED!

HE DID?

YUP! ALL OF YOUR FRIENDS WANT TO KNOW IF THEY CAN DO A SLEEPOVER HERE TONIGHT.

CAN THEY? CAN THEY?

OH, I DON'T KNOW. I THINK THAT'S A LOT TO ASK OF MISS SWAN.

OH, QUITE TO THE CONTRARY!

THE MORE THE MERRIER!

YAY!

WHY ARE YOU SO EXCITED ABOUT THIS?

ARE YOU SURE IT'S OK?

YES! IT'LL BE A GREAT CHANCE TO MEET EVERYONE.

OK. IF YOU'RE FINE WITH IT, THEN SO AM I.

I CAN'T WAIT!

LET'S MAKE SURE YOU HAVE EVERYTHING FOR TONIGHT. YOU'LL BE STAYING IN OUR EXTRA ROOM.

I'M SO HAPPY CHARLIE IS COMING OVER!

WHY DOES IT MATTER TO YOU?

NO REASON!

46

CHAPTER 2

DING DONG!

HELLO, THERE . . .

H-HI. WHO ARE YOU?

CREAK

I'M THE NEW NANNY. YOU CAN CALL ME MISS SWAN.

AND YOU ALL MUST BE MATTHEW'S FRIENDS! PLEASE COME INSIDE.

UM . . .

WEL COM

I'M NOT SUPPOSED TO BE WITH STRANGERS. I'M NOT SURE IF I CAN STAY.

IT'S OK, CHARLIE. I'VE CONTACTED ALL OF YOUR PARENTS ABOUT MISS SWAN. THEY SAID IT WAS FINE.

OH, GOOD. THANKS, MS. R.

MATTHEW, YOUR FRIENDS ARE HERE!

HEY, MATT!

WE THOUGHT WE'D COME CHEER YOU UP.

I BROUGHT SCARY MOVIES!

HEY, GUYS. SOUNDS FUN.

OH, WHERE ARE MY MANNERS? LET ME INTRODUCE YOU TO MATTHEW'S FRIENDS.

THIS IS MARIO . . .

CHARLIE . . .

AND TEO . . .

HELLO!

HELLO, BOYS. IT'S NICE TO MEET YOU.

HI, CHARLIE!

UM . . . HI, JUDY.

HEH-HEH.

WHAT?

I HAVE TO LEAVE FOR WORK! THANK YOU SO MUCH FOR STARTING TONIGHT, MISS SWAN.

OF COURSE!

I HOPE YOU BOYS HAVE A FUN NIGHT!

THANKS, MS. R!

WE'LL DO OUR BEST NOT TO DESTROY YOUR HOUSE. MINIMAL DAMAGE, PROMISE.

I SURE HOPE SO.

MISS SWAN, CAN YOU MAKE THE KIDS SOMETHING FOR DINNER?

I'LL TAKE CARE OF EVERYTHING!

MATTHEW, YOU INCLUDE YOUR SISTER! OK? LET HER PLAY WITH YOU IF SHE WANTS.

YAY!

AW, MAN.

NO COMPLAINING! YOU TAKE CARE OF EACH OTHER.

ALL RIGHT, ALL OF YOU BEHAVE AND HAVE FUN! I'LL TRY TO GET OFF WORK EARLY! BYE!

BYE, MOM.

CLICK

52

UH, MISS SWAN? WHAT ARE YOU GOING TO MAKE FOR DINNER?

YOU CAN EAT WHATEVER YOU LIKE!

WHOA, REALLY?

ABSOLUTELY.

JUST CLEAN UP AFTER YOURSELVES. YOU ALL HAVE A LONG NIGHT OF FUN AHEAD . . .

I'LL BE IN MY ROOM IN CASE ANYTHING HAPPENS.

YEAH!

ARE YOU READY, MATT? I'VE PUT TOGETHER A LIST.

WE'RE GONNA HAVE THE . . .

BEST SLEEPOVER EVER!

NO, IT'S OK. IT'S JUST BEEN REALLY HARD . . .

I'M SORRY I HAVEN'T CALLED.

IT'S OK. WE GET IT. RUBY WAS AWESOME. WE MISS HER TOO.

WELL, WHAT DO YOU THINK OF MISS SWAN? SHE SEEMS PRETTY COOL! I MEAN, SHE LET US EAT WHATEVER WE WANTED.

I DON'T KNOW. SOMETHING DOESN'T SEEM RIGHT ABOUT HER.

WHY? SHE'S NICE ENOUGH.

AND SHE'S LEFT US ALONE!

MY MOM DOESN'T GET IT. I DON'T WANT SWAN TO BE HERE! AND I DON'T CARE IF MOM HAS TO GO BACK TO WORK.

NO ONE CAN REPLACE RUBY.

THAT'S WHY WE THOUGHT HAVING A SLEEPOVER WOULD BE FUN! MAYBE IT'D HELP TAKE YOUR MIND OFF THINGS? HELP YOU MOVE ON?

MOVE ON?

WHY DOES EVERYONE KEEP SAYING THAT? I DON'T WANT TO MOVE ON!

EVERYONE WANTS TO FORGET ALL OF THIS HAPPENED.

WHOA! I'M SORRY, MAN! THAT'S NOT WHAT I MEAN.

WE JUST WANT TO BE HERE FOR YOU IS ALL.

KNOCK! KNOCK!

I'LL GET THE DOOR.

HEY, JUDY.

HEY, GUYS!

HI, CHARLIE!

UM, HI, JUDY . . .

AGAIN.

YOUR GIRLFRIEND IS BACK . . .

WHAT DO YOU WANT?

CAN I PLAY WITH YOU GUYS, PLEASE?!

WE DON'T WANT TO PLAY WITH YOU. GO AWAY!

NO!

MOM, SAID YOU HAVE TO INCLUDE ME! IF YOU DON'T, I'LL GO TELL MISS SWAN!

SLAM!

I DON'T CARE! TELL HER.

IT'S OK, JUDY. YOU CAN HANG OUT WITH US.

NO, GO AHEAD. TELL HER. SHE HASN'T LEFT RUBY'S ROOM ALL NIGHT.

I CAN'T WAIT TO TELL MOM ABOUT HER. SHE'S USELESS.

MOM'LL FIRE HER ON THE SPOT.

UHHH . . . MATT.

HELLO, CHILDREN.

OH JEEZ!

I-I'M SORRY, MISS SWAN.

FOR WHAT?

NOW THAT I'VE SETTLED IN, I WANTED TO MAKE YOU A TREAT!

WHAT KIND OF TREAT?

KRAA!

AND HERE YOU ARE!

OH YES!

THANK YOU, MISS SWAN!

MY FAVORITE . . .

CHOCOLATE-COVERED POPCORN!

YOU KIDS TAKE A SEAT! I HAVE BOWLS FOR EVERYONE.

DON'T HAVE TO TELL ME TWICE.

I'M SO EXCITED.

RUBY USED TO MAKE THIS FOR US! IT WAS OUR FAVORITE.

I KNOW. A LITTLE BIRDIE TOLD ME.

I PUT SOMETHING EXTRA IN THERE FOR YOU . . .

I USED TO LOVE MAKING TREATS FOR MY DAUGHTER AND HUSBAND.

WHAT DO YOU MEAN YOU "USED TO"? DID SOMETHING HAPPEN TO THEM?

OH . . . THEY'VE PASSED AWAY.

IT'S HARD TO LOSE SOMEONE YOU CARE ABOUT.

I'M SORRY.

IT'S . . .

IT'S OK. THANK YOU.

YOU KNOW WHAT? I THINK SOMETHING IS WRONG IN YOUR BOWL, JUDY.

LET ME FIX THAT FOR YOU.

OK.

I'M SORRY.

IT'S OK. SALT JUST ISN'T GOOD FOR MY DIET.

FINISHED!

CAN I HAVE MORE, PLEASE?

OF COURSE!

YOU SHOULDN'T BE MAKING THIS! THIS WAS RUBY'S TREAT FOR US!

EXCUSE ME?

IT'S OK, MATT! IT REMINDS US OF HER!

YEAH!

ALSO, IT'S DELICIOUS!

NO!

WHO DO YOU THINK YOU ARE?!

HEY!

OH! THIS *IS* GOOD!

HELP!

HELP!

AND WE'RE JUST GETTING STARTED.

CLICK!

WHOA!

MATT!

ARE YOU OK?

IT WAS SWAN!

THE BATHROOM, IT WAS THE WOODS!

THE BATHROOM? IT LOOKS NORMAL TO ME.

IT WASN'T! I WAS IN THE WOODS, AND SWAN--

MISS SWAN? SHE WAS IN THE KITCHEN WITH US THE WHOLE TIME . . .

WE THOUGHT YOU WERE DYING.

YEAH, MAN. YOU JUST STARTED CHOKING.

YOU SCARED US, MATT!

CLICK

ARE YOU OK?

SHE'S THE WITCH . . .

WHAT?

MISS SWAN IS THE WITCH OF THE WOODS!

WE'RE SO SCREWED . . .

I THOUGHT I HEARD RUBY'S VOICE, BUT THERE WERE BIRDS EVERYWHERE . . .

BUT YOU SAID THAT WASN'T THE WITCH!

BESIDES . . . I DON'T THINK MISS SWAN IS A MONSTER. I THINK SHE'S JUST SAD ABOUT LOSING HER FAMILY.

YOU KNOW WHO ELSE'S FAMILY DIED?

WHO?

THE WITCH! SHE LOST HER FAMILY TOO.

MAAAAATT!

SLAP!

MARIO!

WHAT? I DIDN'T GO INTO THE WOODS!

WHAT IF YOU DIDN'T SEE WHAT YOU THINK YOU SAW IN THE BATHROOM?

I'M NOT MAKING THIS UP! I PULLED A FEATHER OUT OF MY MOUTH!

WHERE IS IT THEN?

I DON'T KNOW!

WHAT MAKES YOU THINK I KNOW HOW MAGIC WITCH FEATHERS WORK?!

LISTEN, DO YOU REMEMBER THAT TIME CHARLIE THOUGHT HE SAW A GHOST HEAD FLOATING OVER YOUR MOM'S BEDROOM DOOR?

YEAH, I REMEMBER. IT SCARED ME SO BAD I COULDN'T STOP CRYING.

THAT'S BECAUSE YOU'RE A SCAREDY-CAT.

THAT'S NOT NICE.

SHUT UP, MARIO! IT WAS TERRIFYING.

GUYS!

THE POINT IS . . . YOUR MIND JUST MIGHT BE PLAYING TRICKS ON YOU.

FOR INSTANCE, IF YOU AND JUDY WENT INTO THE WOODS, WHY DID NOTHING HAPPEN TO JUDY?

YEAH, YEAH . . . JUDY WAS FINE THE WHOLE TIME.

I DON'T KNOW.

SEE?

NO, WAIT. SWAN DID SOMETHING TO JUDY'S POPCORN, REMEMBER? SHE TOOK IT AWAY AND BROUGHT BACK A NEW BOWL. SHE ONLY POISONED ME!

BUT WHY? SHE'S SUPPOSED TO COME AFTER BOTH OF YOU.

I DON'T KNOW!

MAYBE SHE'S GOT A SOFT SPOT FOR CLINGY LITTLE GIRLS?!

HEY! I DIDN'T DO ANYTHING WRONG! I DIDN'T EVEN WANT TO GO INTO THE WOODS!

YOU KNOW WHAT I THINK?

WHAT?

I THINK YOU'RE JUST SAD . . .

YOU'RE SAD BECAUSE RUBY'S GONE, AND YOU'RE TAKING IT OUT ON MISS SWAN, MOM . . .

. . . AND ME.

THAT'S FINE! BECAUSE I THINK YOU'RE ANNOYING!

YOU'RE ALWAYS BEGGING ME TO PLAY WITH YOU OR GIVE YOU A HUG! BUT YOU KNOW WHAT? I DON'T WANT TO, OK?!

I WANT YOU TO JUST *LEAVE ME ALONE!*

MATT, CALM DOWN.

OH! AND WHY ARE YOU OBSESSING OVER CHARLIE ALL THE TIME?

HE DOESN'T LIKE YOU, OK?!

DO YOU, CHARLIE?

NO.

SEE? NO ONE WANTS YOU AROUND. SO GO AND PLAY BY YOURSELF.

YOU KNOW . . . EVER SINCE RUBY DIED, YOU'VE BEEN NOTHING BUT MEAN TO ME!

I MISS MY BROTHER.

I MEAN, I LIKE YOU, JUDY! I JUST DON'T "LIKE LIKE" YOU!

SLAM!

AW, MAN.

DANG, MATT. THAT WAS ROUGH.

YEAH, MAN. THAT WASN'T COOL.

I DON'T CARE! WE'RE ALL TRAPPED INSIDE THIS HOUSE WITH A WITCH, AND YOU'RE WORRIED ABOUT ME HURTING JUDY'S FEELINGS?!

MISS SWAN'S THE WITCH AND WE NEED TO DO SOMETHING ABOUT IT. WHO'S WITH ME?

WHOA! NO WAY, MATT!

WHAT ARE YOU EXPECTING US TO DO?

I'M NOT BEATING UP AN ADULT!

SHE'S NOT HUMAN!

MARIO, HELP ME TALK SOME SENSE INTO HIM!

MATT, I'M NOT SAYING SHE ISN'T A WITCH, BUT WE SHOULD JUST CALL YOUR MOM.

YEAH, BEFORE WE COMMIT ASSAULT, CAN WE PLEASE TALK TO YOUR MOM?

OK. YEAH, LET'S DO THAT.

MAYBE SHE'LL COME HOME NOW AND TELL MISS SWAN TO GO AWAY.

HE YELLED AT ME, AND HE'S BEING SO MEAN TO MISS SWAN.

JUDY!

WHAT ARE YOU DOING?!

I'M TELLING MOM ON YOU!

HERE. MY MOM WANTS TO TALK WITH YOU.

I DON'T KNOW IF YOU'RE A WITCH, BUT I'M SORRY ABOUT WHAT HAPPENED TO YOUR FAMILY.

I BET YOU MISS THEM A LOT.

YES.

YES, I DO.

YOU'RE A SWEET GIRL.

JUST LIKE MY DAUGHTER.

YOU KNOW WHAT, MATT?

I'M SAD RUBY IS GONE TOO, BUT I'M NOT GOING AROUND MAKING EVERYONE'S LIFE MISERABLE.

YOU KNOW . . . WHEN MY GRANDPA DIED, IT REALLY HIT ME HARD. MY PARENTS GAVE ME HIS OLD CROSS NECKLACE AS A REMINDER . . .

OF HIM, I GUESS . . . IT HELPS ME FEEL LIKE HE'S STILL NEAR TO ME. THAT HE'S IN HEAVEN AND I'LL SEE HIM AGAIN ONE DAY.

A REMINDER OF WHAT?

MAYBE THAT THING CAN BE THE SAME FOR YOU?

YEAH, MAYBE . . .

GUYS, I'M SORRY I'VE BEEN WEIRD ALL NIGHT.

IT'S OK, MATT. WE JUST WANT TO MAKE SURE YOU'RE OK.

YEAH, MAN. LOOK, MAYBE SWAN ISN'T THE WITCH. AND MAYBE SHE IS, BUT . . .

WE'VE GOT YOUR BACK. WE ALWAYS DO.

I WAS JUST SITTING THERE FISHING AND THE DUCKS SWAM UP TO ME, SO I GAVE THEM SOME BREAD.

I DON'T KNOW WHAT IT WAS, BUT SOMETHING ATE ONE OF THE BABY DUCKS!

OH, I HAVE AN IDEA OF WHAT IT WAS.

WHAT?

RIGHT THERE. LOOK!

A SNAKE?!

MM-HMM! A NASTY ONE TOO. VENOMOUS.

BUT WE HAVEN'T HAD ANY SNAKES IN OUR POND THE WHOLE TIME WE'VE LIVED HERE.

IT PROBABLY MADE ITS WAY HERE FROM THE WOODS.

THOSE WOODS ARE NASTY. LOTS OF DANGEROUS THINGS OUT THERE. YOU NEVER KNOW WHAT MIGHT COME CRAWLING OUT.

BUT IT JUST ATTACKED THAT BABY DUCK.

WHAT ARE WE GOING TO DO ABOUT IT?

I DON'T FEEL SAFE FISHING OUT HERE NOW.

HMMM . . . LET'S GO INSIDE.

WHAT IF IT BITES ME OR JUDY?!

DON'T YOU WORRY . . .

WE'LL TAKE CARE OF IT.

CHAPTER 3

THAT MAKES NO SENSE. THE FACT THAT IT IS INDESTRUCTIBLE IS WHAT MAKES IT SO TERRIFYING!

SURE, BUT LISTEN: EVERY MONSTER HAS TO HAVE A WEAKNESS. IT DOESN'T EVEN MATTER IF IT MAKES SENSE OR NOT.

SO VAMPIRES, RIGHT, WHY ARE THEY AFRAID OF GARLIC? THAT'S DUMB!

STAY AWAY!

ALSO, WEREWOLVES CAN ONLY BE KILLED WITH A SILVER BULLET.

EVEN IN *JAWS* THE ONLY WAY TO KILL THE SHARK WAS APPARENTLY TO BLOW IT UP WITH AN OXYGEN TANK.

NOM! NOM!

WHICH WOULDN'T EVEN WORK IN REAL LIFE, BY THE WAY. WE JUST BELIEVE IT BECAUSE THAT'S WHAT THEY TOLD US.

WHO SAYS IT WOULDN'T WORK?

IT'S SCIENCE! YOU CAN'T BLOW UP AN OXYGEN TANK WITH A BULLET! BUT IT DOESN'T MATTER. IT'S A MONSTER, AND TO KILL A MONSTER YOU HAVE TO FIND ITS WEAKNESS.

FINE, I CONCEDE.

OF COURSE YOU DO. MY MONSTER KNOWLEDGE IS SUPREME.

SO, ON TO THE NEXT MOVIE?

LET'S SEE WHAT I BROUGHT.

I ALREADY KNOW WHAT I WANT TO WATCH.

VAMPIRE HUNTER D!

OH YEAH! I DEFINITELY GOTTA SHOW YOU THAT.

THIS SOUNDS LIKE THE COOLEST THING EVER!

IT'S AWESOME!

I HOPE THERE'S A LOT OF BLOOD AND--

AW, MAN! WE'RE OUT OF SNACKS!

BEEP

VRRRRR

JUST DO IT. SHE DESERVES IT!

BUT I DON'T WANT TO. SHE'S DIFFERENT.

MOM, IS THAT YOU?

101

ANIME IS THE COOLEST THING I'VE EVER SEEN. AND I HATE YOU, TEO, FOR KEEPING IT FROM ME FOR SO LONG.

MATT, YOU OK?

I WAS RIGHT . . .

BOOM!

RIGHT ABOUT WHAT?

THOOM!

CRASH!

BACK UP, GUYS!

I DON'T WANNA DIE!

I DON'T WANNA DIE!

HEHEHEH.

OH, MAN.

SHE SMELLS TERRIBLE!

YOU BRAT!

MATT? WHAT'S GOING ON?

JUDY, RUN!

ATTACK!

MARIO! WHAT ARE YOU DOING?!

SAVING YOUR BUTTS! GET AWAY FROM THE WINDOW!

CRASH!

AHHH!

OOF!

THWACK!

MARIO!

SO WHAT NOW? IS SHE JUST COMING BACK?

UGGHHN

MARIO! ARE YOU OK?

I THINK SO. MY HEAD HURTS.

WHERE'S SWAN?

I SMACKED HER WITH A BAT. SHE'S OUTSIDE SOMEWHERE.

SWAN?

THAT THING WAS MISS SWAN?

YEAH, MATT WAS RIGHT!

ALL THE WINDOWS ARE CLOSED AND DOORS ARE LOCKED.

I CAN'T BELIEVE THIS IS HAPPENING . . .

HOW IN THE WORLD IS THIS ALL REAL?

I TOLD YOU GUYS MY BROTHER WASN'T LYING.

I CAN'T BELIEVE IT EITHER. MISS SWAN WAS NICE TO ME.

YEAH, WELL. SHE'S A MAN-EATING MONSTER.

JUST LIKE I SAID SHE WAS. I'M CALLING MY MOM!

WHERE DO YOU THINK SWAN IS?

I DON'T KNOW.

CRAP!

WHAT IS IT?

THE LINE IS DEAD.

WHOA! LOOK . . .

SHE CUT THE CORD.

ARE YOU KIDDING ME? WHAT DO WE DO NOW?

MAYBE WE COULD RUN FOR HELP. CHARLIE IS PRETTY FAST.

NO WAY, MAN! I'M NOT LEAVING. SHE'S OUT THERE!

I DON'T THINK RUNNING FOR HELP WOULD WORK . . .

SHE'S WATCHING US. I'M SURE OF IT.

DO YOU THINK SHE'S GOING TO EAT US?

I HOPE NOT, BUT YEAH . . .

PROBABLY.

NAH, MAN. SHE'S JUST AFTER MATT AND JUDY. WE DIDN'T GO INTO HER WOODS.

MAAATT . . .

I DON'T WANT TO BE EATEN.

MARIO, REALLY?

NO, MARIO IS RIGHT. WE NEED TO KNOW HOW THIS WORKS.

MARIO, TELL US EVERYTHING YOU KNOW ABOUT THE WITCH?

WHAT? THOSE ARE THE RULES, MAN!

SHE STILL THREW YOU INTO A WALL.

I--I JUST KNOW THE BASICS. I DON'T EVEN KNOW IF IT'S ACCURATE.

IT'S FINE, JUST TELL US ANYWAYS.

SIGH

OK . . .

HERE'S WHAT MY BROTHER TOLD ME . . . HE SAID IT ALL BEGAN OUT IN THE WOODS, A LONG TIME AGO . . .

LEGEND HAS IT, HER FAMILY LIVED IN THERE LONG BEFORE ANYONE ELSE SETTLED IN THE AREA.

SWAN WAS AN ORDINARY WOMAN. SHE HAD A YOUNG DAUGHTER AND HUSBAND. AND THEY LOVED LIVING THERE.

THE WOODS WERE FULL OF RAVENS, AND THE FAMILY FORMED A SPECIAL CONNECTION WITH THEM.

EVENTUALLY MORE PEOPLE SETTLED NEAR THE AREA.

THEY WERE AFRAID OF THE WOODS, TELLING TALES OF THE BIRDS THAT WERE POSSESSED BY EVIL SPIRIRTS.

SO WHEN A GROUP OF KIDS FOUND SWAN'S DAUGHTER PLAYING WITH THE BIRDS . . .

KRAA!

. . . THE KIDS RAN HOME AND ACCUSED THE FAMILY OF WITCHCRAFT.

THE VILLAGERS BELIEVED THE KIDS AND RETURNED TO CONFRONT THE FAMILY, BUT SWAN WAS NOT THERE.

SHE RETURNED HOME TO FIND HER FAMILY, DEAD.

SHE WENT MAD WITH GRIEF . . .

AND DISAPPEARED INTO THE WOODS . . .

BUT SHE FOUND SOMETHING IN THOSE WOODS . . .

KRAA!

AND THE BIRDS OFFERED HER SOMETHING . . .

I THINK SOMETHING ELSE IS GOING ON HERE . . . SHE'S HAD HER CHANCE TO KILL US, BUT SHE HASN'T . . .

ARE WE COMPLAINING ABOUT THIS?

NO, BUT WHEN I FOUND HER OVER JUDY, SHE DIDN'T SEEM LIKE SHE WANTED TO HURT HER.

SHE DIDN'T SEEM TO HAVE A PROBLEM COMING AFTER YOU.

YEAH, MAN. WE'VE GOTTA DO SOMETHING. WE CAN'T JUST WAIT FOR SWAN TO GET US.

IF SHE DECIDES TO COME BACK INTO THIS HOUSE WE'RE ALL DONE FOR.

WE NEED A PLAN.

DO YOU SEE IT?

SEE WHAT?

THERE IN THE GRASS, CLOSER TO THE WATER.

I SEE IT! THE SNAKE IS BACK!

YEAH, IT IS . . . I SET SOME BREAD OUT FOR THE DUCKS TO LURE HIM IN.

BUT WHAT ABOUT THE DUCKLINGS?

DON'T WORRY ABOUT THEM.

YOU WAIT HERE.

BUT--

HM. THAT'S NOT TRUE . . . MONSTERS LIKE THIS AREN'T COMPLICATED.

THEY'RE SNEAKY AND OPPORTUNISTIC. THEY'RE LOOKING FOR SOMETHING THEY THINK IS WEAK . . .

AND WHEN THEIR PREY ISN'T LOOKING . . . THEY STRIKE . . .

IT'S THEIR INSTINCT.

USE THAT AGAINST THEM . . .

. . . AND YOU CAN DEFEAT A MONSTER LIKE THAT ONE DAY.

WHAT IF WE WAIT THINGS OUT? EVENTUALLY MS. R WILL COME HOME AND WE CAN GET HELP THEN.

IT CAN'T BE TOO LONG UNTIL SHE'S HOME, RIGHT?

BUT WHAT IF IT IS? OR SWAN JUST ATTACKS MS. R AS SHE'S COMING INSIDE?

I DON'T WANT MY MOM TO DIE!

GUYS! ENOUGH! WE HAVE TO DO SOMETHING NOW. IF WE JUST KEEP WAITING HERE, SWAN WILL EVENTUALLY COME BACK.

WHAT ARE YOU SUGGESTING?

I SAY WE GO OUT THERE AND START THE FIGHT.

UH, ARE YOU CRAZY?!

YESSSSS!

MY KIND OF CRAZY!

CLANG!

HERE'S WHAT I FOUND.

THIS IS IT?

YUP.

I DON'T LIKE OUR ODDS.

EVERYONE, WATCH OUT!

WHOA!

I GRABBED EVERYTHING I COULD THINK OF.

WHAT IS ALL OF THIS?

MONSTER WEAPONS!

I'M TELLING YOU, MAN. IF WE'RE GOING TO KILL A MONSTER WE HAVE TO KNOW ITS WEAKNESS.

A BAT ACROSS THE FACE WORKED PRETTY WELL LAST TIME.

OK, SO WHAT'S THE PLAN?

A LITTLE WHILE AGO RUBY KILLED A DANGEROUS SNAKE IN OUR BACKYARD.

SHE USED THE DUCKS AS BAIT AND THEN AMBUSHED THE SNAKE. I'M THINKING WE DO THE SAME.

WE LURE SWAN IN WITH SOMETHING SHE WANTS AND ATTACK HER, CATCHING HER OFF GUARD.

SO WHAT ARE WE SUPPOSED TO USE AS BAIT?

OH.

WHAT?

LISTEN, YOU TRUST ME, RIGHT?

YES . . .

GOOD.

YOU'LL BE OK.

SO, LISTEN . . . YOU'RE JUST GOING TO WALK OUT THERE TOWARD THE WATER, SHINING YOUR FLASHLIGHT.

THE REST OF US ARE GOING TO SNEAK AROUND THE HOUSE. HOPEFULLY SHE WON'T SEE US COMING. WHEN SHE COMES DOWN TO GET YOU, WE'LL SURPRISE HER. OK?

OK.

GOOD LUCK, JUDY. YOU'LL BE OK!

I DON'T CARE WHAT YOU THINK!

OHHHH, DANG, CHARLIE!

COME ON, GUYS. LET'S GET INTO POSITION.

GOOD LUCK, JUDY!

KRAA!

GASP

JUDY!

DID THAT BIRD SAY MY NAME?

MISS SWAN!

WHY ARE YOU DOING THIS?

KRAA!

KRAA!

ALL RIGHT, COME ON, GUYS!

YOU KNOW . . . ALL OF THIS MONSTER HUNTING STUFF IS A LOT MORE FUN IN MOVIES.

SAYS YOU.

THIS IS RAD!

SHHH!

WE HAVE TO KEEP QUIET. SWAN CAN'T SUSPECT WE'RE HERE.

JUDY!

JUDY!

OK, I'M READY TO GO INSIDE NOW.

MATT! I DON'T THINK THIS IS A GOOD IDEA!

YOU'RE FINE! BE BRAVE!

I DON'T WANT TO DO THIS!

MOM! WATCH OUT!!!

KRAA!

AHHH!

GET THEM!

MISS SWAN, STOP ALL OF THIS!

JUDY, WHAT ARE YOU DOING?

NO, YOU'RE JUST LIKE ALL THE REST OF THEM!

NO, I'M NOT! I'M SORRY I WENT INTO YOUR WOODS!

I WAS TRYING TO DO SOMETHING RUBY SHOWED ME WHEN SHE GOT RID OF A SNAKE IN THE BACKYARD. I THOUGHT IT WOULD WORK!

RUBY WOULD NEVER TELL YOU TO PUT YOUR SISTER AT RISK LIKE THAT.

SHE ALWAYS PROTECTED YOU!

YOU'RE RIGHT . . . I DIDN'T KNOW WHAT TO DO AND RUBY ALWAYS DID.

I THOUGHT MAYBE SHE WAS TELLING ME SOMETHING . . .

I WAS WRONG . . .

RUBY ISN'T TALKING TO ME . . .

SHE'S JUST GONE.

I'M SORRY TOO . . . I HAVEN'T TRIED TO UNDERSTAND HOW YOU'RE FEELING.

I SHOULD HAVE BEEN THERE FOR YOU. I'VE JUST BEEN SO WORRIED ABOUT GETTING BACK TO WORK.

BUT THAT DOESN'T MATTER NOW.

WHAT?

WHY?

I QUIT.

YOU DID?!

YES. THEY SHOULDN'T HAVE BEEN PRESSURING ME TO COME BACK.

I'LL FIGURE OUT A NEW JOB. WE'LL BE FINE.

RIGHT NOW YOU TWO NEED ME . . .

AND JUDY . . . SHE DOESN'T KNOW HOW TO SAY IT, MATTHEW . . .

SHE'S NEEDED YOU TOO.

AND RUBY ISN'T GONE. SHE'S STILL WITH US . . .

HER LIFE AND *ALL* OF THE LOVE SHE HAD FOR US . . . THAT STAYS WITH US FOREVER . . .

WE JUST HAVE TO REMEMBER.

BOOM!

MATTHEW, WAKE UP . . .

NNNH . . . RUBY?

WHAT'S THE MATTER? IS EVERYTHING OK?

WILL YOU COME SIT WITH US?

WE'RE SCARED!

YAWN

OK. I'M COMING.

WHEN IS MOM COMING HOME?

DON'T KNOW. IT WAS A BUSY NIGHT AT THE RESTAURANT.

BOOM!

OH GOODNESS . . . HOW FAR AWAY DO YOU THINK THAT ONE WAS?

FIVE MILES . . . I COUNTED THE SECONDS.

IT SOUNDS CLOSER NOW.

HOW DO YOU KNOW?

YOU COUNT THE SECONDS FROM WHEN YOU SEE THE LIGHTNING STRIKE. EACH SECOND IS A MILE.

IS THAT TRUE?

BOOM!

OH NO. THAT ONE WAS FOUR SECONDS.

MATT, NO! THIS ISN'T A GOOD IDEA. GO GET HELP.

IT WON'T MATTER. WE DON'T HAVE TIME, AND COPS DON'T GO INTO THE WOODS.

JUDY'S DOOMED WITHOUT OUR HELP. THIS IS OUR ONLY CHANCE TO GET HER BACK.

BUT WE DON'T EVEN KNOW SWAN'S WEAKNESS.

WOULD YOU SHUT UP ABOUT WEAKNESSES?

THAT'S DUMB MOVIE STUFF, MAN! WHAT IF WE'RE IN *ALIEN* AND NOT *ALIENS*?!

NO, WE NEED TO KNOW WHAT HER WEAKNESS IS BEFORE WE CAN FIGHT HER!

I THINK WE *DO* KNOW WHAT IT IS . . .

WHAT?

THAT THING? IT'S JUST A SOUVENIR!

NO, I THINK IT'S SALT.

I CUT HER WITH THIS OUT AT THE POND, AND IT HURT HER. IT'S MADE OF SALT . . .

SLICE!

OH YEAH! AND REMEMBER, JUDY OFFERED HER SALT ON HER POPCORN EARLIER? SWAN WAS SCARED OF IT.

WE CAN DO THIS. WE CAN STOP HER. WE KNOW HER WEAKNESS . . .

SEE, THEY ALWAYS HAVE A WEAKNESS.

WHATEVER.

SO WHAT NOW?

WE'RE JUST A BUNCH OF KIDS. AND SHE'S A MONSTER WITH AN ARMY OF EVIL RAVENS!

WE'RE GOING TO MAKE AN ENTIRE ARSENAL OF SALT WEAPONS!

SALT

WE GET TO BE FOR REAL MONSTER HUNTERS?

I HAVE SOME IDEAS . . .

I'M GONNA HELP!

FINE. I'LL COME TOO.

WE'RE ALL GOING TO DIE.

YUP.

WE GET TO BE MONSTER HUNTERS!

SO WHAT ARE YOU THINKING?

WE'LL FILL ALL OF THE SUPER SOAKERS WITH SALT WATER.

I LIKE WHERE YOUR HEAD'S AT!

BUT WE'RE GOING TO NEED MORE . . .

WE CAN CREATE SALT GRENADES WITH PLASTIC WRAP . . .

YOU THINK WE MADE ENOUGH?

SHE DOESN'T STAND A CHANCE.

WE SHOULD BRING PLENTY OF EXTRA SALT WITH US JUST IN CASE.

WE'LL BE IN THE DARK, SO WE'LL NEED LIGHTS.

AND IF ALL ELSE FAILS, I HAVE THIS . . .

CHAPTER 4

IT'S HER BACKPACK FOR SURE.

I REMEMBER THE BUTTERFLIES ON IT . . . AND HER RED SHOES.

DO YOU THINK SHE'S DEAD?

YES.

SNIFF

MATT, ARE YOU OK?

WE NEED TO END THIS, ONCE AND FOR ALL . . .

KRAA!

DID YOU KNOW RAVENS ARE CONSIDERED MESSENGERS OF THE DEAD?

OR AN OMEN OF DEATH . . .

SWAN SHOULD HAVE NEVER COME TO THIS PLACE . . .

WHAT WAS THAT?

THUMP!

JUDY?! IS THAT YOU?!

JUDY!

MATT, WAIT! MAYBE WE DON'T JUST RUN DEEPER INTO THE SCARIEST HOUSE ON EARTH!

GET OFF HIM, WITCH!

I'M NOT DONE WITH YOU BOYS YET!

YOU DON'T WANT TO MESS WITH US. WE KNOW YOUR WEAKNESS IS SALT, AND *WE'RE GOING TO END YOU.*

KA-CHIK!

AHHH!

CRUNCH!

IF YOU EVEN THINK OF SHOOTING, I'LL TEAR HIM LIMB FROM LIMB . . .

SO I SUGGEST YOU DROP IT.

MATT, DON'T LISTEN TO HER! TAKE HER OUT!

OK, YOU WIN!

JUST DON'T HURT HIM!

WHY ARE YOU LISTENING TO HIM? HE DOESN'T CARE ABOUT YOU. EVER SINCE RUBY DIED . . .

. . . HE'S NOT EVEN HUGGED YOU.

JUDY, I'M SORRY!

THEY DON'T LOVE YOU. THEY JUST WANT YOU OUT OF THE WAY.

BUT I DON'T . . .

I WANT YOU TO JOIN MY FAMILY.

I WANT YOU TO BE MY DAUGHTER . . .

AHHHH!

HER DAUGHTER!

JOIN US!

OUR FAMILY!

RAHHH!

GIVE IN TO YOUR CHANGE, JUDY.

FORGET WHO THEY ARE . . .

THEY DON'T CARE ABOUT YOU, AND WHEN YOU'RE LIKE ME YOU CAN PUNISH THEM TOO . . .

THAT'S WHY I'VE KEPT THEM ALIVE . . .

THEY'LL BE YOUR FIRST HUNT!

I SHOULD HAVE BEEN THERE FOR YOU. REMEMBER WHEN WE USED TO SIT TOGETHER WITH RUBY DURING THUNDERSTORMS AND IT MADE YOU FEEL BETTER?

I'M SITTING WITH YOU NOW. REMEMBER WHAT RUBY TAUGHT US . . . *I LOVE YOU!*

MATT . . .

THOOM!!!

COME ON!

RELOAD!

YEARGH!

YOU . . .

STAY AWAY!

RAHHH!

SOMETHING TERRIBLE HAPPENED TO YOU, EVEN WORSE THAN MY FAMILY LOSING RUBY. BUT YOU FORGOT THEM . . .

IT WAS WRONG, WHAT HAPPENED TO YOU. WRONG THAT THOSE KIDS TOOK YOUR FAMILY. WRONG THAT EVERYONE LEFT YOU TO YOUR PAIN . . .

YOU SAID YOU WERE FREE FROM YOUR PAIN, BUT LOOK AT WHAT YOU'VE DONE BECAUSE OF IT!

LOOK AT WHAT YOU'VE **BECOME** BECAUSE OF IT.

YOU'VE FORGOTTEN THE HOPE YOUR DAUGHTER GAVE YOU AND WHAT YOUR FAMILY TAUGHT YOU . . .

YOU AREN'T THE PERSON THEY LOVED. YOU'VE FORGOTTEN THEM . . .

NO . . .

I'LL ALWAYS BE THERE FOR YOU WHEN A SNAKE SHOWS UP IN OUR POND . . .

. . . OR ANY KIND OF MONSTER.

SHE'S GONE AND SHE'S NEVER COMING BACK!

NO!

YOU'RE WRONG!!!

SPLIK!

AHHHH!

I WANT YOU TO BURY THAT DEEP INSIDE . . .

SHE'S NEVER GONE! AS LONG AS I REMEMBER!

ONE MONTH LATER

OH, MAN! I CAN'T BELIEVE I'M FINALLY PLAYING THIS!

ALTERED BEAST IS LIKE FIVE YEARS OLD, CHARLIE!

I KNOW, BUT I WAS ALWAYS TOO SCARED TO PLAY IT BEFORE.

THIS NEW VERSION OF CHARLIE IS SO WEIRD.

HE FIGHTS A MONSTER AND GETS NEW GLASSES, NOW HE'S A TOUGH GUY.

POWER UP!

OH SWEET! MY MUSCLES ARE BIGGER NOW!

KNOCK! KNOCK!

WAIT UNTIL YOU TURN INTO A WOLF!

I GET TO TURN INTO A WOLF?!

I'LL GET THE DOOR.

HEY, JUDY.

BREAKFAST IS READY.

THANK YOU FOR THE BREAKFAST.

I'M SO GLAD YOU BOYS ENJOYED IT.

COME ON, TEO!

THANK YOU, MISS AUDREY!

FACE YOUR DOOM!

OH, MAN! WE'RE AT THE BOSS!

IT'S NOT HARD! JUST HIT HIM, JUMP, AND DASH!

YOU OK, MATT?

YEAH. I THINK SO.

IT'S JUST . . . SO MUCH HAPPENED. AND I REALLY LIKE AUDREY . . . BUT SHE'S NOT RUBY.

NO ONE EVER WILL BE! RUBY WAS AWESOME AND SPECIAL.

I KNOW.

I JUST DON'T WANT TO FORGET HER.

THE END

Color flatting assistance by Viviane Regina, Story Regina, Kev Brett, Savana Byrne, Renea Fractor, and Journey Regina

SPECIAL THANKS TO:

My awesome wife, Viviane, and kids, Story, Journey, and Shepherd, for their support and understanding as I've chased this crazy dream of making comics. My mom, Renea Fractor, for believing in my dreams as a little kid and jumping in to help me realize them as an adult.

My amazing agent, Elena Giovinazzo, and everyone at Pippin Properties. Chris Hernandez at Razorbill for helping me turn this idea into a book I'm really proud of. Jessica Jenkins for her art direction and that awesome logo design!

Josh Ulrich, Stephen McCranie, Kazu Kibuishi, Mike Maihack, Jason Brubaker, Brian Russell, and Wes Molebash for being great friends and cartoonists who supported this project from the beginning. Matt Nelson for pushing me to make custom brushes.

The real-life Ruby for being amazing to us kids—we miss you. Jennifer Blackmar for being a great sister, even when my friends slept over. Chris, Jei, and Michael, who made childhood a lot of fun. To all of my family and friends, who constantly support me with their love and kindness.

To Christ, who is always with us, even when things are hard.